DEAD MAN WALKING

A NICK HOLLERAN BOOK

DAVID GREEN

Available from Black Hare Press

SHORT READS

WARDENCLYFFE by GREGG CUNNINGHAM
HADES 11 by PAUL WARMERDAM
BLOOD AND SILK by ZOEY XOLTON
AS ABOVE, SO BENEATH by JOSHUA D. TAYLOR
THE RISE OF THE GREAT OLD ONE by JASMINE JARVIS
DEAD MAN WALKING by DAVID GREEN
CHRYSALIS by KIMBERLY REI
MOUNT TERROR by E.L. GILES
HELL HATH NO FURY by CHISTO HEALY
THE RECKONING by STEPHANIE SCISSOM

UNDERGROUND

MIRACLE GROWTH by TIM MENDEES
THE RETURN by GABRIELLA BALCOM
UNDERGROUND by STEVEN STREETER
WHISPERS IN THE DARK by K.B. ELIJAH
SWIRLING DARKNESS by SAM M. PHILLIPS
THE GATE TO THE UNDERWORLD by E.L. GILES
COLD AS HELL by NEEN COHEN
THOSE OF THE LIGHT by NICOLA CURRIE
TIME'S ABYSS by JAMES PYLES
UNDERWORLD GAMES by JONATHAN D. STIFFY
PLACE OF CAVES by CHARLOTTE O'FARRELL
AFTER THE FALL by STEPHEN HERCZEG
BEYOND HUMAN by MATHEW CLARKE
THE FALL OF PACIFICA by M. SYDNOR JR.

ISBN 978-1-925809-80-0

Edited by D. Kershaw
Formatting by Ben Thomas
Cover design by Dawn Burdett

Twitter: @BlackHarePress
Facebook: BlackHarePress
Website: www.BlackHarePress.com

For Ollie. Hope your dad makes you proud.

x
David, November 2020

TABLE OF CONTENTS

PROLOGUE

Might say life changed the day I died.

Can't say I saw it coming, but as I breathed my last, I came to terms with it. A bright light warmed me as I floated above my body. A pang of regret shot through my conscience as rivers of blood slid from three bullet holes in my chest, turning the white shirt I wore crimson. The regret grew when a

11

woman raced towards my prone body, pressing her hands and jacket to the wounds, holding the precious blood inside that sack of meat and bones.

The light that beckoned me with gentle love stopped calling. I hovered there between life and death—not wanting to go back, but unable to move on. Paramedics arrived on the scene in record time and coaxed my body back to life. An undesired miracle.

What happens to a man once he knows God is real? That if a stranger had gone left instead of right, I'd have bled out in an alley crammed with filth and joined Him in the afterlife?

On the day I left the hospital—after operations, recuperation, and a bill I'll be paying for the rest of my second life—I discovered Hell exists too.

We're living there.

SPECTRES OF THE PAST

SEPTEMBER 20th, 2024
HAVEN CITY, OREGON

It's been five years to the day since I died.

Looking through my office window, I raise a
tumbler of Jack Daniel's to the grey heavens.

"Hey big guy, it's Nick Holleran. Here's to ya,

13

you sonofabitch."

The drink goes down well. I'm not an alcoholic. That's what they all say, right? Here, it's true. Liquor would be an easy crutch to lean on, and a drunk private investigator too perfect an image. Maybe I'll sink towards a walking cliché at some point down the road, but not today. Have to keep my wits about me.

In the corner of my office, an adolescent girl stands with her back to me, staring into the corner. I noticed her when I returned here after being shot and left for dead in that alley. Could've stood there for years. She's never spoken a word to me. I asked her where her parents were and pulled her round to face me.

Her eyeless stare sent me scrambling backwards. Congealed blood crusted her cheeks, and her mouth hung open and slack. In silence, she resumed her study of the wall.

14

No one else sees her. I ignore her now. Part of the furniture.

When I returned to life, I discovered an unfamiliar world. It's funny—the Pacific Northwest contains the highest number of atheists in the USA. I used to be an "aggressive nonbeliever," a label stuck on me by my dear mother.

Now, you could say I'm a zealot. The afterlife exists; Heaven is up there, waiting for some of us after we die. Thing is, Hell isn't below our feet. Maybe there are seven layers, like Dante wrote, but I know this for sure. Hell is Earth. I see them everywhere I go. Ghosts, demons, and anything else I read about in a bible or storybook. Some know they're here and can affect the living. Others don't. The myths and legends you've read about? Real. Every one.

Including Bigfoot. I know…I talked to the guy.

Sighing, I rub at my chest scars under my shirt and turn away from the girl. Back to the window. Nirvana's song "Scentless Apprentice" crunches out of the speakers on my desk. Listen, I'm from Oregon. Grunge music is in my blood, and I enjoy rewinding to my teenage years. Everyone has a little stereotype in us. It's getting dark outside; a light rain floats on the air, swirled this way and that by the Fall wind. Down on the sidewalk, a woman in a sanitary mask, hood drawn up, pauses and glances up at my window before ducking in through the entrance. I fill my mouth with Jack Daniel's again. It's a Friday.

You might wonder why I continue to do the PI work after I know the truth. It's like this—I want to go upstairs when I die. Can't kill myself, I've seen too much to realise the priests and fanatics were correct about suicide. So, I help people, and I try to figure out an answer to the greatest question: why

16

did humanity wind up in Hell? Is this how it's always been? Did we deserve our fate? So far, I've got nada.

Footsteps outside my office door tell me the woman's about to enter. She hesitates…they always do. I flick off Nirvana, ready to give the client my full attention. I glance at the girl in the corner; don't think she's a fan of grunge—not that she's ever complained, but maybe it's the way her shoulders slump even more when I listen to it. There are folk like me out there, but I've had to search to discover them. Our "talent" isn't something we like to shout about; the people who talk end up under care. Each time someone enters my office, I wonder if they'll be able to see her too.

The door swings open and in she walks. Tall, and I guess dark-haired, though it's tough to tell with her hood drawn up. Eyes filled with brown pools peer at me over the top of her sanitary mask.

17

The woman's wearing gloves too, like it's the height of Covid-19's first or second wave. She pauses next to the ghost in the corner, and for a second, I hold my breath.

"Nick Holleran?" she asks, her voice muffled by the mask.

"You understand there hasn't been an outbreak for three years?" I say, pointing to the chair opposite my desk. "Don't worry though, the seat's at least two metres away."

Her eyes narrow at my remark, but she sits down anyway. Staring at me, she strips off the gloves, her hands are red—scarred and puckered flesh like acid stripped the original layer away. Next, the mask comes off, and even though I half expect what I'll see, my heart goes out to her.

A scar runs from cheek to cheek, straight through her mouth. Her lips look chewed up, she resembles a Picasso. I raise my gaze to those

18

beautiful eyes of hers, and she looks back without flinching.

"Are you done with the wise guy routine?" she asks, her speech revealing missing teeth. It ain't from some accident; someone's tortured the woman, used her flesh like a canvas. I nod.

"You are?"

"That can wait, you'll understand why. I want you to hear me out first."

I glance at my computer screen, and an email from a source in the Haven Police Department is open, detailing any recent strange cases or ones declared "cold." Something about this woman tickles my mind. Grabbing the bottle of Jack Daniel's, I refill my glass and pour some into another for her. She offers me a slight smile, her scars pulling tighter, and takes a sip.

"How can I help you?" I ask, holding the tumbler in my hand, not consuming it. I've found over the years other people will drink easier if I join them, and this woman looks like she could do with one.

"Someone is following me," she replies in an even tone. She tosses the hood from her head, her hair is thick and luscious—a wave of chocolate running down to her waist.

"Don't take those sorts of cases," I reply with a laugh. I reach for a cigarette but have second thoughts. Smoking can wait. "Tried the police?"

"I can't do that," she replies.

There's something here, beneath the surface that's pulling at me. I get walk-in clients, but more often I find a case on myself or the PD turn to me when they've exhausted their possibilities. It's the paranormal, the supernatural, I work on now. Not that the boys at the precinct call them that. Haven't worked a straight case since the guy I got paid to tail left three holes in my chest. But…

"Any idea why someone would want to follow you?"

She takes another sip.

"I could think of a dozen reasons, and that doesn't concern me. It's the who that bothers me."

"Wait," I say, leaning back in my chair. "You're not 'concerned' about being followed?"

"No," she offers, giving me that tight smile again. "It's expected. I've always been careful and can see the signs. Sometimes it's comforting, knowing someone is watching you. But not this time."

I roll my eyes and spin my chair, taking a glance out of the window. On the sidewalk, a man stares at my window with no pretence.

"Case solved," I say, turning back to her and throwing a thumb over my shoulder. "There's the perp, on the sidewalk. Either he's got sloppy, or you ain't all that at looking."

21

The woman springs to her feet and strides to the window, gripping the ledge and narrowing her eyes as she scans the sidewalk before making an annoyed noise in her throat.

"Where?" she bites out. "The sidewalk's empty."

"There," I reply, pointing down at the figure. It's then I realise my mistake.

The rain doesn't trouble him. Instead, it appears to fall around and through him. I squint. Can't make out his face, but his skin and the clothes he's wearing look drained of colour, like cheap fabrics put through too many washes and dry cycles. Just like the girl in the corner.

The woman returns to her seat and crosses her legs, looking like the cat that got the cream and a little extra on top.

"So, what I've heard about you is true," she says. It's my turn to take a drink.

"Who do you think is following you?" I ask, tapping a finger against my desk.

"My husband."

"When did he die?"

"Four weeks ago," she replies without blinking, "and he's been trailing me ever since. I didn't notice him for the first week, just a chill— that sensation when eyes fix on you. Then the presence grew. I can't explain it, but I sense him everywhere. It fills me with fear."

Silence falls, except for the pitter-patter against my window. A thought batters against my brain, but I don't want to listen to it.

"Huh," I breathe, just to say something. I know there's a question I should ask, but my tongue doesn't want to.

"Is it true what they say? That spirits stay when they have unfinished business?" She motions at her glass with a gnarled finger. I refill it. Mine

23

too.

"Kinda," I reply, my admiration of the woman increasing with my intrigue. She's done her research and having her suspicions confirmed doesn't make her fly into a panic, though I can tell by the tightness around her eyes it's a facade. She's scared. "The dead fade if they meet a purpose they stuck around for. Others need forcing away, if they've turned malevolent. Others just...hang around."

"Ask your question, Mr Holleran. I can see it on the tip of your tongue."

"What's your name?" I ask, a weight pressing against my chest. *He* died a month ago. The man who killed me.

"My name is Michelle Wheeler."

"Wheeler?" I say, the bullet wounds in my chest pinning me to the back of my chair.

"Yes, my husband's Dean Wheeler."

It's five years ago, and I'm back in this alley again. Dean Wheeler headed down here and didn't come out. Place is a dead-end. I turn, and there he stands. Gun pointing at me.

"Who hired you?" he asks, taking a step forward.

"Don't know what you're talking about," I reply, holding my hands above my head. I knew I shouldn't have followed him in here, but a big payday awaited and I got impatient.

"Last mistake you'll ever make, friend."

Wheeler pulls the trigger. The muzzle flashes, the gunshot echoes, but I feel no pain. I glance down and see smoke drift from my chest, blood turns my white shirt red. Then the pain hits. Another gunshot. This time the agony is instant as I fall onto my back.

Tears trickle from my eyes as I stare at the stars. Wheeler stands above me and smiles. He aims the gun at my chest and fires for a third time.

Michelle Wheeler watches me; the tumbler of Jack Daniel's held to her lips. I never saw the woman when I worked the Wheeler case, though I'd heard her name. A simple job, or so I thought. I'd cut corners and paid the ultimate price. Or I should have done, if it wasn't for Rosa—the woman who'd held the blood inside me, who'd dialled 911. I haven't spoken to her in too long.

I turn to my window. The ghost's face is clear now. Dean Wheeler's vacant eyes peer up at me.

My mind's wandered, and I pull my thoughts back to the matter at hand.

"You know your husband shot me?" I asked. It wasn't a well-known fact. When I could, I told the cops it'd been a mugging gone wrong. Dean Wheeler had his fingers in Haven's organised crime. In deep. Even in the state Wheeler had left me in, my employers, a rival crime family, wouldn't have wanted me blabbing. They sent me a bottle of twenty-year-old whiskey, a bouquet, and a ten-thousand-dollar cheque for services rendered. I haven't cashed it. Wheeler never bothered with me since. The bug crushed underfoot—guess I never mattered much to him. Revenge crossed my mind, but it's a sin. I've seen Heaven, and I want a place there when I pass.

"Yes," she replied, placing the glass on my desk. "You see why I ruled out the police? I need you to find out why his ghost is following me. Can you do it?"

"That depends," I reply, looking out of the window while I consider my next words, half expecting to see Dean Wheeler looming behind me. He isn't there, and his spirit's vanished from the sidewalk, too. Some dead are aware straight away, others grow into it. Looks like Wheeler is strengthening. "Why would your husband want to haunt you?"

27

"Let's see," Michelle answers, leaning forward and placing her hands in front of me. "He tortured me, and worse. He needed to possess me in life. Why should that be different in death?"

She stays where she is, staring with such an intense heat. I give two fucks to politeness and pull out a cigarette, taking my time to light it. That first inhale is exquisite.

"Listen," I say after blowing smoke towards the ceiling. "This could get worse. If he's hurt you before, *you* could be his unfinished business. Dean could stay a regular ghost—harmless. But if he strengthens, meaning his personality returns and he can affect the living, I'd fear for your safety."

I'm surprised at my fervour. I can't get the image of Dean gunning me down, and this damaged woman in front of me is spurring me on.

"There's little time is what you're saying," she says, biting her top lip. "Will you help me?"

28

"It's gonna cost you. I ain't cheap, and I have to work fast. Wheeler may be here for a reason— and I must find what that is—or he may be one who needs convincing. That's messy, and it's a last resort."

"Money isn't an issue," she breathes. I notice her shoulders droop as tension leaves her body. There's more to this case than she's letting on.

"It is for some, sweetheart," I say, sliding over a piece of card and a pen. "I've not said I'll take the job yet. I've another client due. Leave me your cell, I'll have more questions for you. Where will you be?"

Michelle held the pen in an awkward grip and scrawled her number, passing it across to me. She holds my stare again. Those eyes.

"Home, I've nowhere else to go. I'll be speaking with you soon," she says as she picks up a card with my number on it, before leaving without a backward glance.

I stare out of the window, smoking my cigarette. Michelle strides down the sidewalk, hood, mask, and gloves back in place.

The girl still stands in the corner, facing the wall. Does she pay attention to my conversations? Does she care what goes on beyond that space? I don't have another client coming: a lie—I wanted Michelle to leave—the excuse a simple way to buy myself time to plan and investigate Dean Wheeler's death.

I know I'll take the case. It's personal.

TROUBLE AT THE STYX

Reaching out to my sources unearthed information. Police ruled Wheeler's death a suicide, but the crew Dean ran with don't believe it. Michelle Wheeler is a person of interest to them— and the local PD is keeping tabs.

The situation stinks.

Then there's the matter of Dean Wheeler.

What does he want? Spirits manifest in unique ways, but all start the same way. There's some instinct that drives them; in Wheeler's case, it's stalking his wife. Some ghosts stay like that—living a half-forgotten echo of their life—like the girl in my office. Others strengthen, and that can get interesting. I'm betting Wheeler will be the malevolent type, and they need dealing with. The rest accept their new existence and enjoy the liberation death grants them. I know one or two.

Going outside is something I hated doing after I died: it took a lot of getting used to. I'd walk with my eyes down, shoulders slumped and narrow, avoiding the living and dead. Now, the scenes are as familiar to me as the bullet wounds in my chest. I stroll past the washed-out figure of a man with a long beard, in his shirtsleeves and braces. He kneels, staring at the palms of his hands, and weeps. That ghost hasn't moved in five years since I first saw him.

Ghosts come and go: it depends on how present they are—the fact Wheeler vanished from the sidewalk is the first sign of awareness. It's normal for them to leave the living to themselves, even the ghosts who are aware. There are exceptions. One guy, Eddy, died in 1927. He doesn't remember why he stuck around; though from some stories he tells, I reckon he enjoyed several of the seven sins. Nice fella…he checks in on his family line once a week. None of them lived when he walked the earth, but a gracious gesture all the same.

I make my way to the Styx Bar. Place is a dive, though the goths love it. Its owner, Ruby, is like me. She died for four minutes as a child, swallowed something she shouldn't have and choked. Course, her old man brought her back, and she's lived knowing the truth since then. Almost sixty goddamn years. I learned a lot from Ruby, and most of Haven's sentient supernatural know the Styx is a safe place for them. Hell, I like the place. Some music played here works for me, and the patrons downstairs are, for the most part, my kind of dead.

The damp heat dogs my steps, and I'm glad to get inside the Styx with its air conditioning. Four or five people are sitting with their beers as an angst-ridden teenager plays acoustic guitar on stage. I smile at the sight of one of the Styx's resident demons, Cyril, sitting in rapt attention. The creature is immense—red and purple scales cover his muscled bulk. His lower teeth protrude from his jaw like tusks. If the human patrons of the bar knew Cyril—I don't know *who* named him—sat amongst them, they'd run a mile and then keep going for one or two more.

Nodding at the barman, I step behind the bar and through a door with a sign that reads: STAFF

ONLY.

What I grew to understand is that the demons, ghosts, and all the creatures of Hell have existed thousands of years. And these folk, just like humans, have their vices. They eat, drink, shit, and curse like the rest of us. They have their own society, with laws in a fashion—I've worked more than one case on behalf of demon kind in the last five years—and just like humans, there are demons I like and assholes. Cyril is the former, but I'm thankful to avoid him as I slink down the stairs to Styx proper—me and his ex disagreed a while back.

Ruby is behind the bar. The joint isn't busy. Two strengthened ghosts I don't recognise are talking by the jukebox—"Helter Skelter" by The Beatles is playing, which would please Charles Manson no end if he knew—and, much to my delight, a Nephilim sits at the bar, nursing a bottle of Scotch.

Nephilims are enormous deals. Haven is home to two of them, and this one's name is Suraz. I've exchanged nods with him and seen the other. They're the saddest creatures I've ever laid eyes on, and seeing as we're all living in Hell, that's saying something. Suraz's raven hair flows to his waist above his gold-plated armour, and his skin is the same colour. I take a seat a few barstools down from him as he glances at me. His deep yellow eyes hold aeons worth of sorrow. I nod, and he inclines his head, before turning back to his bottle.

Rosa used to say I held too much sadness in my blue eyes for her to stand, sometimes. That seems a long time ago.

Anyway, if anyone would know the answers to the questions that plague me—Hell on Earth and why—a Nephilim would know. Problem is, they don't do a lot of talking, and when they do, it's not to answer questions from the likes of me.

"Holleran," Ruby says with a wink. She'd been gazing at Suraz. Easy to understand; a Nephilim's beauty surpasses all else. "Long time, no see. What can I get ya?"

"Coffee, please," I reply, slipping my jacket off. "What's new?"

"Plenty. Wendigo sightings out in the country. Notice the sky seems darker at night time than it used to? Red during the day, too. Something's in the air, Holleran."

Ruby moves to the coffee machine. She's tall, about five-foot ten, with bright pink hair at odds with the deep wrinkles around her eyes and on her forehead. Ruby pulls it off, though—she's what I imagine a sixty-six-year-old PJ Harvey would be. I take another glance at Suraz. His unfocused stare into the bottom of his Scotch bottle suggests he's centuries away.

"Working a fresh case?" Ruby asks, placing

black coffee in front of me.

"Maybe," I say. "What've you heard about Dean Wheeler's death?"

"Wheeler? The punk who shot you?"

I nod. I sense Suraz shift—out of the corner of my eye, I can see him watching me.

"Yeah, the one and fucking only. Heard he'd died four weeks back but tried to ignore it. His widow came to me today, suspected of being followed by her dead husband. Wasn't wrong; Wheeler's spirit tracked her to my office. Hasn't strengthened yet, but you can bet this whole joint he will, and the cocksucker will be trouble."

"Wait," Ruby says, holding her hands up. "How'd she know Wheeler trailed her? Could she see him?"

I do a double-take. The ghosts of my past with Wheeler had clouded my thought process. How had Michelle Wheeler known?

"That's a damn good question," I say, looking at Ruby—but she's staring beyond me.

An iron grip squeezes my collarbone and I'm lifted into the air, flung into the far wall. The breath escapes my lungs in a *whoosh*, and the impact of my side against the concrete breaks at least one rib. Before I realise what's happening, I'm picked up and pressed against the wall.

Cyril's four eyes, black and glinting, are inches from mine. His furious breath fills my nostrils. He holds me with one hand, and he presses the claws of his other into the stubble on my neck.

"Cyril," I say. "Long time, no see."

"Fuck you," the demon barks. "Why did you do that to Francis?"

I figured this might be a problem, being the reason I hadn't darkened the Styx's door for a while. See, Francis and Cyril were familiars. Not lovers like in human terms, it's deeper than that. A few months back, worked a case about girls of a similar look and age going missing around Haven. Turns out old Francis sacrificed them, looking for a way to speak to Lucifer himself—I'm told it's possible, but haven't come across a soul who's done it. Satan keeps to himself these days.

"Did what I had to, Cyril," I snarl, inching my fingers towards the revolver at my waist. Normal bullets wouldn't do much against a demon—but those dowsed in holy water pack a punch. "He murdered six girls. I know you don't want to hear that, but Francis left me no choice. I had to Expunge him."

It isn't what he wants to hear. With a growl, he draws his claw back, ready to tear my throat out.

"Stop."

It's like a whisper, but the command reverberates inside my head, almost to the point of pain. My fingers had found the revolver's handle, but they stay there, unable to move. I look past Cyril and see my saviour, Suraz, standing as tall as the monster holding me.

"Is this true, demon?" he asks. In his hand is a golden blade the length of your average human male.

Cyril snarls but has no choice but to answer.

"Yes," he bites out. "But Expunging? He's gone, Nephilim. Forever."

For a moment, I pity the demon. I could never comprehend his loss. My empathy ends as Cyril takes a swipe at me.

Suraz is faster. Like a blur, he drives his golden blade into the demon's back and through his chest. Ichor covers my blond hair, turning it black and smelling of sulphur. Cyril's grip loosens, and I fall to my knees. The demon copies me, and a second later, his decapitated head bounces to the ground, his tongue lolling between his tusks and his lifeless eyes staring towards Heaven.

"Some advice, human," Suraz murmurs, his whispers beating at my skull. "You play a dangerous game with our world, but I see in your eyes you cannot stop. Tread with care. Ruby is correct. Something *is* amiss, and it troubles me."

With that, the Nephilim turns and strides for the exit. I look at Ruby across the ruin of the demon's body in front of me. She sighs and points at the dead beast.

"The Nephilim killed my best fucking customer. Help me clean this mess up, Holleran."

ILL OMENS

Cleaning up after a Nephilim impales then decapitates a demon of Hell is just as fun as it sounds.

"So, Dean Wheeler," Ruby says. I grunt in reply. We've talked little since Suraz made the beast a head shorter. Thick black blood stains the floorboards, and I'm covered in it. Its sulphuric

43

smell lingers and puts ideas of gagging into my mind. Ichor crusting into my hair and skin is not a pleasant sensation.

"Yeah," I say, in the hope speaking may distract my nose. "Dean fucking Wheeler. Had a job to follow him five years back, didn't get much on him, then tried to forget the sonofabitch after. You know anything?"

Ruby stands with a sigh and rolls her neck while working her shoulders.

"This fucking blood'll be staining these floors for weeks," she says, tossing her mop into the filth-encrusted bucket. "Heard a bit. Who hasn't? The Wheeler family is notorious, reckon they know him as far as Seattle. What'll concern you is, two or three years back, he snooped around upstairs, bothering Guz about some 'secret' bar for 'certain' types of folk. Dean took an interest in the occult, I'm told. They say suicide, but a prick like him? No, not buying it."

"This is getting too fucking interesting," I mutter, reaching for a cigarette and lighter. I tried vaping after I died for a while, but what's the point? "Makes sense. Someone had clued Michelle into our world, and she suspected her dead husband of following her. Question is—why? It's been a matter of weeks, so Wheeler's spirit is still working on instinct. Don't think I want to leave it till he strengthens to find out what he desires."

"That leaves the wife," Ruby says with a nod.

"Yes, it does," I drawl. "She knows more than she's letting on. My guys tell me the cops *and* Wheeler's old associates are watching her too. Think I need to pay her a visit. Want me to stay and help more?"

Ruby laughs. It's a sound full of heart—she always looks on the bright side of Hell.

"Go. You've not done much more than spread

poor Cyril's blood around the place. Poor fucker, affable guy for a demon." I stand with a grimace that's almost a smile and retrieve my jacket. Ruby calls after me as I head for the stairs. "Nick? If the state of Hell worries a Nephilim, I'd be extra careful out there. Something has him spooked."

Spooked. Good one.

"Thanks Ruby, see ya around," I say with a wink.

***

My smartphone tells me it's just past 10 p.m. Michelle Wheeler should be at her home, and lucky for me I know where that is. I staked the place out once or twice five years back—it's an enormous mansion on the outskirts of Haven. The boys in the precinct told me it's still the Wheelers' address. Intuition tells me not to travel there yet. Ruby's right: if a Nephilim's worried, things are in danger of going south.

I have Michelle's number. It'd be easy to call her, but I want to look into those beautiful eyes of hers when she lies to me again.

Two million people live in Haven and many more dead. With a population that size, there's a good number of folk who shared experiences like mine and Ruby. Others know, too—an enterprising person here who figured it out against the odds, or a knowledgeable individual here whose information got passed down through the family. The latter's who I need to confer with, and I know the guys. I flag down a passing taxi and climb in, murmur the address I want, and let my thoughts focus on the Wheelers.

It bothers me Dean's dead. A part of me wanted to be the one to kill him. Too much heat, and now Heaven is real, I want to save my place. The excitement at the prospect of Expunging him, like I did with the demon Francis, worries me even more. It might have to perform it—but it requires the right reason. Acting for the sake of it, without just cause, is murder.

I know I'm not above the urge for revenge, but Expunging is more than that. Picture the universe is a rug, made up of a multitude of cotton threads of equal importance. Every person in Hell, alive or not, is a thread. Expunging one removes that piece from the entire makeup: it's wiped away, stopped from ascending to Heaven or remaining in Hell. Sometimes, it's required—but doing it too much could cause the entire rug to unravel. I can't imagine the big bastard upstairs or his friend down here being too happy about that.

The worst part is the vision in the Expunged's eyes when they realise. They've peered into oblivion, and the endless void stares back.

***

Arriving at my destination, I linger outside as I stare at a name and number on my smartphone: Rosa's. The woman who kept the blood inside my chest and called 911. I'd have ascended to Heaven if it weren't for her. We became close after, though it didn't work—I couldn't sort my feelings out about her role in my resuscitation and life afterwards.

Rosa knows the truth; I told her everything.

I press the call button, then the coward inside me hangs up—not fast enough—my phone vibrates, and it's Rosa ringing back.

"Nick?" I hear her voice filled with concern as I press the phone to my ear.

"Hey Rosa, sorry must have pocket dialled you."

A beat of silence.

49

"Right…well, nice hearing from you, Nick."

"Wait," I say, with too much desperation. "That's a lie. Guess I wanted to hear your voice, is all."

"Nick, what's going on? I haven't heard from you in about a year; now you're lying about calling me at 10:30 p.m. on a Friday night? Are you drunk?"

I laugh, but it's a little strained.

"Sorry, I wasn't thinking." I pause… I can hear her breathing and the soft murmur of her TV playing in the background. I bite the bullet. "Dean Wheeler's dead."

"Good," she replies with heat.

"That's not all. His widow approached me. He's following her, but something doesn't feel right. Her story doesn't add up."

"No shit," Rosa says. I can picture her ebony head shaking at my dumbness. "That's a little coincidental, don't you think? I know that sonofabitch wouldn't let death stop him from being a scumbag, but are you sure you ain't getting played?"

The air's grown chill over a matter of seconds, and I can see my breath hanging in the air. I glance around; I'm alone in the deserted street.

"No," I say. "But you shoulda seen his wife. He did awful things to her, and I don't want more blood on my hands if I can help it."

"Are you sure you aren't seeking revenge?"

A shiver runs through my body. Not at Rosa's words—I've been pondering them myself—but at the cold. Frost glints on the sidewalk beneath my feet. I smell trouble.

"Look Rosa, I gotta go," I say. Her garbled voice chops in and out of reception in my ear until my phone beeps, telling me it's out of coverage. Mist oozes from the asphalt, and the trouble I

51

sniffed before is pungent.

Drawing my revolver helps my stomach unclench, but I know I'm under-prepared. My holy water-doused bullets will only work against certain Hellspawn, and as my mind races to tell me what manner of creature could affect the weather, a figure padding out of the fog confirms my worst fears.

"Well, shit," I mutter as I pull out what might be my last cigarette. It isn't just for pleasure.

Amaroks hate fire, and though the amount my cigarette and lighter emits is small, it's all I've got.

There's a plus side—unlike normal wolves, an Amarok hunts alone. I'm not thanking my lucky stars yet—this beast is the size of a small pony. Its red eyes glint at me through the gloom; saliva drips from its razor sharp fangs—the liquid sizzles when it meets the floor.

"Mind if I finish this?" I ask, holding my cigarette up between two fingers.

The Amarok howls. It's blood curdling. You know that sensation when you wake in the middle of the night startled and afraid, but you don't know why? That's one of these bastards howling close by. A normal human doesn't *hear* it, but on some level they *feel* it.

As the cry dies down, another answers, and it's too close for comfort. I spin around and sitting twenty feet behind me is another Amarok.

"Well, fuck me," I say, tossing my cigarette to the ground. I hold my lighter high and aim my revolver at it. Realisation floods in—I'm shit outta luck.

"Dean Wheeler sends his regards," the newcomer growls, the words awkward in its maw.

I've no time to think…the wolf to my left lets out a snarl and pounces. Leaping backwards, I snap my aim in its direction and let off a round, fighting the urge to keep firing—there's only so many bullets. The Amarok changes direction mid-air to avoid being hit and lands with a gymnast's grace on its four legs.

Despite the cold, I tear off my jacket and light it before tossing it to the ground. It flames with speed, and I circle it as I attempt to keep the conflagration between me and the Amaroks. They're intelligent creatures, but their lone-wolf instincts play in my favour—they seem confused at the prospect of working together.

I add to the confusion. I run at one, lighter in hand, like a desperate Olympic torchbearer. The Amarok scrambles backwards, and changing direction, I spin and fire at the other. My bullet strikes home, grazing its cheek and embedding itself in the massive wolf's left shoulder. It lets out a pained yelp as steam rises from the wound—the holy water doing its work. The hit won't kill it, but it'll slow it down.

Grinning, I let my guard down too long as the other Amarok recovers and bounds onto my back. I hit the ground and roll, needing to keep as much space between them as I can—as the sizzling asphalt shows, an Amarok's saliva could burn through my flesh, never mind their fangs and claws.

But I've lost my advantage. The injured Amarok sends me spinning as it charges past me, clipping me enough to send me onto my back.

As my revolver and lighter spin from my grip, I realise I'm fucked.

The Amaroks approach, the flames of my burning jacket dying behind them. I close my eyes, hoping it'll be quick and that Heaven still waits for me.

A warm glow washes over me, and my eyes snap open. The monstrous wolves shrink back as a figure steps over me. I laugh, and it's one of relief. Perhaps I'm not ready to die again yet.

"About fucking time!" I cry. It's Maeve, a strengthened ghost, and one of the people I came to visit.

Her presence fills the street, chasing away the Amarok's frost. My oppressors whimper, their mighty tails between the legs. They ain't beaten yet. The injured wolf nips at the other, urging it forward. They're intelligent creatures and know a strengthened ghost has limits. The Amarok steps forward.

A projectile collides into it, bursting into flames. The beast howls as its fur burns, the stench of cooking flesh fills the air. It looks at the Amarok with the bullet wound in desperation as it collapses, its bones turning to liquid from the heat. The monster melts before our eyes. Its partner flees without a backward glance.

I struggle to my feet, my cracked rib from earlier making its presence known among my fresh bumps and scrapes. The burning Amarok is now a steaming puddle of blood, marrow, and fur. Maeve watches me, and I nod to her.

"Thanks," I say. "Maybe don't leave it too late next time?"

"Had to prepare the grenade," a voice calls. It's Harry, Maeve's husband. He's alive but comes from a long line of "truthers"—people who've known the truth about this world for generations. Harry's a healthy eighty-seven. He and Maeve died in a car accident back in the sixties—he came back to the land of the living, and she didn't. Maeve waits for him: they're so in love they want to ascend to Heaven together. I envy them.

"Much obliged," I mutter, my fingers itching for another cigarette. I sigh as I remember they were in my jacket.

"Two Amaroks!" Harry cries, slapping me on the shoulder. I wince. "Unheard of, my boy. A fine battle."

I shake my head, scanning around for my revolver.

"No," I say. "Way too easy. They shoulda killed me without a struggle. Let's get inside, we need to talk."

OCCULT'S A DIRTY WORD

"Dean Wheeler," Harry says with a whistle. "If he can bend Amarok to his will, four weeks dead, then I'd hate to see what he'll do in another month."

We're sitting inside the old man's study and I've given him and Maeve the blow-by-blow of the day. I shake my head at that thought—so much

59

drama. Just hours ago, me and the ghost in my office were relieving my teenage years listening to Nirvana. Now, I've watched as a Nephilim decapitated a demon I didn't dislike, and hunted by a pair of Amarok.

"What do you think Wheeler wants with you, Nick?" Maeve asks, her translucent stare kind and wise. She's a beautiful ghost, looking the same as she did sixty years ago when she died. "It's obvious he's trying to use you for something. You intend on confronting him?"

I flick my eyes around the room. The study holds ample books for a library. I love visiting the pair; the area is a treat, filled with curios gathered over a lifetime. The fireplace is a pleasant touch, if careless with all the paper scattered around. Harry's family researched Hell and its creatures for centuries. The old man continued the tradition, but his line will die with him. Harry reminds me of Doc

60

Brown from the *Back to the Future* movies—he has the same crazy white hair and wild look in his eyes. From the way he looks into Maeve's youthful face, I can tell he never gave a second thought about moving on from her.

"I do," I say, answering Maeve's question. "Sometimes the best way to spring a trap is to walk right into it. Ruby at the Styx mentioned Wheeler and the occult."

"Pah," Maeve would have spat, if she could produce saliva. "That's a dirty word, you know better than that."

I hold up my hands and wince, recognising my mistake. The denizens of Hell object to the word "occult"—they say it has negative connotations, and they ain't all bad.

"All right," I say with my most charming smile, a lopsided one that makes me look boyish and disarming. I think. "Sorry, you know what I meant.

He'd researched Hell before he died, is what I meant."

"Interesting," Harry muttered, stroking the white stubble on his chin. "Things are strange in Hell. Two Amaroks hunting together is proof of that. Then you had your case of the demon summoning Lucifer. Unpleasant business— ridiculous, too. How did Wheeler die?"

"Suicide is the official word."

Harry and Maeve share a glance. It speaks volumes, and I don't like it.

"Shoot," Harry says, getting to his feet. I marvel at how spry he is. "Didn't offer you a drink. Tea, coffee, something stronger?"

"Coffee," I reply, winking at him. "Think it's gonna be a night."

Harry laughs and heads for the kitchen, leaving me alone with his wife. I try to pinpoint when I became so at ease in the dead's presence but realise it doesn't matter. They've always been around—I just couldn't see them.

"So Dean Wheeler committing suicide is a problem," I say. It isn't a question: their reaction made it clear.

"How's Rosa?" she says instead. "Seen much of her?"

I take a quick look at my smartphone. Eleven missed calls from her. It makes me feel... wanted? Making a mental note to call her back as soon as I can, I point at Maeve.

"Don't change the subject. His suicide is bad?"

"Yes. Consider most people, when they die, have no idea about reality. Then they either ascend or stay in Hell in some form. Some, like you, get a second chance. But then, there're folk like me—aware of all this," Maeve says, spreading her arms wide, "before they pass. If a man like Dean Wheeler

63

prepared for this, then he's dangerous. Look at the speed of his strengthening. He's a cruel man who strives for domination. Being dead takes what he can do to a whole extra level."

Harry shuffles back in, holding a tray laden with biscuits, teapots, coffee, and everything that goes with it. He places it down with care in front of me. I think for a second as I pour out a little cream, enjoying the crackling and popping from the fire. The warmth is comforting.

"Harry," I begin, "it's a last resort, but the Amarok attack changes things. It's clear Wheeler knows his wife spoke to me and wants me out of the picture. He's planning something for her, and my only option left might be to Expunge him tonight."

Maeve shudders. Ghosts carry over tics like that from when they were human. It's like muscle memory, without the muscles. Harry nods.

"Two left—you must bring me more

ingredients to craft more."

He moves to his bureau and unlocks a drawer with a key kept around his neck. The Expungers are inside. Palm-sized, the devices are flat. I can make them, but Harry likes to keep busy. Gathering the ingredients is the arduous part—some are straightforward enough to gather like garlic and holy water, mixed in with liquid iron. The last item is the dangerous one—fae blood and wings. Now, these aren't fairies like Tinkerbell from the children's stories. They're vicious, sadistic terrors that delight in human suffering. I don't enjoy Expunging, but I'll gather the required items if it means there are less fae in Hell. I suppose I must answer to Lilith herself one day—if Hell's taught me anything, it's that everything comes with a price.

Harry hands them to me. They're harmless to the living, but my fingers tingle when I touch them. Hangover from my near-death experience.

"I'm thinking this isn't a straightforward haunting with intent to harm," I say, looking at Maeve, then Harry. "Let's track this. A proper piece of work delves into the—sorry, Maeve—occult, then commits suicide. What's the angle?"

"Sacrifice," Harry mutters with a shiver. I do, too. The air is frigid again, and I notice the flames in the fireplace are dying.

"There's powerful magic in sacrifice. The stronger the connection between the victim and the aggressor, the more potent the spell."

Maeve freezes. It's like she's a video and someone's hit pause.

"Honey?" Harry says, standing in front of her and peering into her eyes. The irises move with frantic jerks. "Nick, can you…"

He doesn't finish. The fire snuffs out, plunging the study into twilight. I grab an Expunger in one hand and my revolver in the other. Green smoke

66

tendrils slither from underneath the door, and dread clenches my stomach. I stagger against a table as my legs tremble. Harry's dropped to his knees, tears cascading down his cheeks.

A hooded figure stands by the study's door. Darkness emanates from him. I know it's a male—my instincts tell me it's Wheeler.

For a second, Hell holds its breath.

Wheeler points at Harry. The old man lifts off the ground, his limbs stiff and splayed like Da Vinci's Vitruvian Man. I attempt to swing my revolver around at Wheeler, but I feel his regard fasten on me and I can't move.

Harry vibrates. Teeth bared and clenched. Blood rushes from his eyes, nostrils, and ears. I want to scream, but my jaw refuses to listen to my command. Instead, I weep as I watch my oldest friend's skin tear away from his body. My ears pop at the sudden intake of air, like Wheeler is drawing it all into him.

Harry implodes. One second he's there, suspended in mid-air, being flayed alive. The next moment, nothing except a pool of blood on the floor.

I blink as a spotlight shines down from above me; my fears and grief wash away as its gentle light warms me. The Gates of Heaven are open, and they're calling Harry home. Squinting, I see his spirit. He smiles at me then looks at his wife and holds out his hand. Maeve's eyes continue to dart and I understand. Harry's ascending, and whatever Wheeler is doing means Maeve can't follow.

I strain, attempt to fight my invisible restraints, but it's no good. The moment my friends have waited for sixty-years is here, and this dead asshole is denying them their eternity together.

"No!" Harry's voice echoes as he drifts upwards towards God's eternal embrace. He wants to stay if Maeve can't follow, but he's being forced upwards, the choice taken away from him.

All I can do is watch as he becomes one with the light, and then it vanishes—gates closed.

Wheeler disappears too, and I fall forwards onto my face. I beat my revolver's handle on the floor and scream my lungs dry.

"Nick."

Maeve's quiet whisper draws my attention. Her tears match mine, but she has a strength I can only wish for.

"I'm sorry," I spit out, kneeling in front of her.

"It's not your fault," she says, looking up at the ceiling as if she hopes her husband can convince Heaven to call to her. My stare falls to a photo frame on the table. I pick it up and look at a black-and-white picture of Harry and Maeve when they were teenagers. Replacing it, I climb to my feet and head for the door.

"What will you do?" Maeve calls after me. I turn.

"I'm gonna find Wheeler," I say, stuffing the Expungers in my pockets, "and make that sonofabitch pay. For everything."

REVENGE IS A DISH BEST
SERVED...HOT

My journey to the Wheeler estate is uneventful. I know he wants me, but I don't care why—first chance I get, I'll Expunge the bastard.

Hell holds its breath—living and dead. The streets are quiet and the damp heat has turned oppressive. My tie is loose and my shirt's top buttons are open, though the heat of the Expungers against my thigh overrides all else. It's like they're eager for action. I share the sentiment.

The Wheeler estate sticks out like a gorilla in a monkey pen. Not for its size, but because of the swirling, green- and purple-hued clouds menacing the sky above it.

There's no sound. It's absent, and it proves unbearable.

I hum a song as I walk the perimeter of the building, and I smile to myself when I realise the tune is "Bullet With Butterfly Wings" by The Smashing Pumpkins—an apt choice as I tap the Expungers in my pocket.

Without a sign of life, the building seems abandoned, but I know something inside is causing the sky to act the way it is. I ascend the steps to the mansion's double-doors and reach out for the handle. It turns in my hand, and my way in is clear.

There's one pressing matter left. I grab my smartphone and select Rosa's profile. Her image beams back at me. I took that photo in better times. Ignoring the ream of missed calls, I send her a text instead.

Rosa, I'm sorry about tonight. There's so much to explain. If you'll let me, I'd like to. Face to face. Nick.

As soon as I press send, I realise how stupid I've been. I might not make it out alive.

The same pregnant pause hangs inside the Wheeler mansion. From my scouting of the exterior, I search for somewhere lower than the ground floor—darkness emanated from each window—and I don't want to waste time scouring every room this house has. I figure a place this size would boast a basement and stalk past the grand staircase to find it.

My quest doesn't last long. Tendrils of green

smoke, matching the ones from Harry and Maeve's study, swirl around my ankles—an ethereal breadcrumb trail showing me the way. It's too easy. My bones know it, but I couldn't give a shit. My blood pumps fire, and my anger demands satisfaction.

The smoke draws me towards a door under a flight of stairs. I press my ear to it and hear the faint sobbing of a female. Pulling my revolver from its holster—a habit, I understand it will be as useful as vomit-flavoured lollipop—I ease the door open and creep down the flight of stairs. The green light grows powerful as I descend, and I bare my teeth with delight at the scene before me.

Michelle Wheeler lies on the floor, cowering at the far side of the green-flamed candlelit room. Standing before her, his back to me, is the washed-out back of Dean Wheeler. My attention snaps on him, and I have no interest in anything else surrounding me. Yanking an Expunger from my pocket, I run towards him.

As I reach him and thrust my arm out, I see Michelle look at me—a smile tugging at the scars on her face.

The Expunger makes contact.

"Die, you fuck!" I scream, pushing against the Expunger, as if I can force it into his matter.

Steam rises from it. Dean Wheeler lurches around to face me. I grin as I stare into his wide eyes. I want him to know it's me that ended him, but Wheeler doesn't see me. The dead man stares into oblivion as realisation dawns on him that the void is his eternal damnation.

His spirit unravels, like invisible hands have found the end of his thread and are pulling on it with all their might. From head down, he disintegrates— and that's when my mistakes hit home.

Michelle Wheeler watches her husband's

Expunging with delight painted across her ruined face. She sees him. Ruby's words slam into my head.

"How'd she know? Wheeler trailed her? Could she see him?"

Only Wheeler's legs are visible, and they're deteriorating. His feet are standing inside a pentagram etched into the ground—and so are mine. I take a step forward, and it's as if I've collided with a wall. Michelle had trapped Dean, and now she's done the same to me. We've both been pawns in Michelle's game. She's played it well.

I didn't spring the trap. I strolled right through its gates, like a sap on a day trip to fucking Disneyland.

Michelle steps around her husband's pentagram, a knife in her hand. The runes flash as she brandishes it, and the pain when she plunges it below my ribs causes me to sink to my knees, held inside the pentagram. My blood trickles into my pentagram and fills it. A line links mine with Dean's.

"When did you die?" I ask. Most would ask "why?" but I figure she'll tell me anyway: the satisfied smile informs me she's the type.

"The first time? A year after you. Dean killed and resuscitated me more than once. It got him off." She spits on where his remains would have lain, but there's nothing there. For a second, I feel a pang of pity for her—even though she's killed me. Murdered by both fucking Wheelers. I chuckle and blow a bubble of blood onto her.

"What's so funny, Mr Holleran?"

"Please," I say, "call me Nick. No need to be formal now you've driven six inches of steel into me. Dean's interest in the occult, your passion I presume?"

"You did your homework," she says. I glance

at her bare feet and notice Michelle takes care not to step on either pentagram. Interesting. "You've earned your reputation for diligence, but there's nothing like revenge and a damsel in distress to make a man stupid."

There's an altar ahead of me. Michelle walks to it in silence, and I listen to her feet slap against the concrete. That's not all; there's a wind howling outside—it's loud enough to make its presence known down here. The basement appears darker, but that might be my vision failing. My bloods fill my pentagram, and the excess floods into Dean's.

Michelle approaches, holding an Expunger.

"The erasing of a spirit as evil as my husband's, by a man he murdered, is a powerful sacrifice. Death links your souls. You know what would be even stronger?"

"Enlighten me," I reply, though I can see what's coming.

"The sacrifice of a soul that's lived twice, tainted by revenge." Michelle crouches, those beautiful eyes staring into mine. "People have dominated me my whole life, Nick. No more. I've discovered a way to be in control. For eternity."

She half reaches out to me, as if to caress my face, but remembers the pentagram.

"You're the key. Thank you for your sacrifice."

I've no idea if it'll work, but I'm out of options.

Smiling my boyish, lopsided grin, I pull my revolver from its holster.

Michelle Wheeler's eyes widen as I aim it at her and pull the trigger. Its blast answered by the splatter of her brains hitting the altar and her body slamming to the ground.

I fall forwards, released from the pentagram. Michelle's foot lays across the lines, breaking the pattern.

"My luck's in," I say out loud for reasons that escape me, and I struggle to my knees. My body aches, it's telling me I haven't got long left.

The wind howls inside the basement as, like clockwork, Michelle's spirit rises from her dead body. No warm glow beckoning her. Revenge is a sin, and even though Dean deserved it, killing him and making it look like a suicide's still murder. I fish my last Expunger from my pocket and toss it at her, looking away—I've no desire to see it carry out its work.

The wind bluster stops, and the green flames die. I crane my neck to stare at the ceiling, hoping they view my deeds tonight as just, or else forgiven, and the Gates of Heaven will open for me.

A second passes.

Then another.

A third.

"You're looking in the wrong direction, you know."

The voice is silk. It's like every accent I've ever heard rolled into one. It's at once intoxicating and terrifying. I can't hold my head up any longer, and it drops, though I stay on my knees.

A figure steps from behind me and crouches to peer into my face. At first, I think he's a Nephilim—his size, skin, and features remind me of Suraz, but his sheer presence tells me he's something more. His stare is like a weight smothering my conscience.

"Lucifer," I cough, blood dribbling down my chin.

Satan smiles and produces the whitest piece of cloth I've ever seen. It's a shame when he presses it against my mouth and cleans away my blood.

"I should thank you," Lucifer says, glancing down at the pentagrams, "I suspect I wouldn't have enjoyed what Michelle Wheeler had in store for me."

"What do you mean?" I ask and sway forwards. The Devil himself holds me upright with the little finger of his left hand.

"These sacrifices weren't something I could ignore, thanks to my Big Brother." He points to the ceiling. "He's a fan of obscure rules and laws— unless they concern him. Anyway, a spell this powerful I'd have had to carry out Michelle's command. Anything within my power, I'd have to act."

"Right." I'm so fucking tired.

"Your brain isn't working as it should, Holleran. Understandable," Lucifer says, tapping me on the cheek with a light touch. It feels like the time Rosa slapped me. "You completed the ceremony when you Expunged Michelle. I suppose you'll want me to heal you?"

Lucifer blows into his palms and rubs them

together.

"Wait!" I shout, a reserve of strength coming from somewhere. "There's a soul trapped here. A good one. She meant to ascend decades ago but didn't—Maeve Wells. Can you do it? Send her to Heaven to be with her husband?"

Lucifer gets to his feet and glances around the room, shock etched into his obsidian features. He crouches again.

"Human, that's the first time I've felt something other than apathy in millennia. You'd do that? You realise those Pearly Gates don't await, you know. When your body gives up in one hundred and ninety-four seconds, you're staying in Hell. In His books, revenge is revenge."

I nod. There isn't a second thought.

"Done," Lucifer says with a thunderous clap.

He stands and looks up at the ceiling. I can see in his eyes he sees straight through it; his gaze goes directly to the heavens.

"This won't do," he says, looking down at me. "You know what? This is my kingdom now, His rules. Fuck Him."

Lucifer crouches and lays his palm against my side. It's like lightning's struck me. He holds me down with his other hand as I gasp and convulse. He lets go and I bounce to my feet, ready to run the New York Marathon.

"Fixed your ribs, too," Lucifer says with a wink. "Now, if that's all? Stay out of trouble, Holleran. One life left."

"Wait," I shout as he moves by me. "I need to know something. Why is the world like this? Why are we all in Hell?"

Lucifer pauses, his back to me. He looks over his shoulder, golden eyes narrowed.

"I suppose there's no harm," he says, turning to face me. I'm reminded of his force of will as his stare penetrates mine. "My brother cast out my supporters from Heaven. That much is true. Back then, there wasn't a Hell. God created it for those who supported me. Humans included." He places a hand on my shoulder. "Your people were always the most loyal. Now you have to prove yourselves before you're let in, and my brother is rather fickle."

With that last word, Lucifer spins and strides into the darkness at the end of the basement. The candles spurt back into life, and I'm left to ponder the Devil's revelations.

EPILOGUE: AFTER...

SEPTEMBER 21st, 2024
HAVEN CITY, OREGON

"Next Friday, then?" I say, pausing for Rosa's reply, flicking my eyes towards the girl ghost in the corner of my office. I wonder if she can hear the excitement in my voice, or if she listens at all.

87

"Okay," Rosa replies, "it's a date. Wear something nice, and no ghost stories please. I don't care how many dead guys are in the restaurant alongside us."

"Have it your way." I laugh. "Deal."

"See you Friday, Nick Holleran."

"Rosa?"

A pause.

"Yeah?"

"Thank you."

"Don't thank me yet, big guy. You suck at first dates." She laughs as she hangs up.

I whoop as I lean back in my chair and reach for my packet of cigarettes. I pull one out and go to light it, staring at the beautiful day outside my window.

"They'll kill you, you know?"

The cigarette hangs from my lip as I turn, dumbfounded, towards the ghost who's haunted my office in silence for five years. I feel flames licking from her eyeless stare as she faces me from the other side of my desk. The cigarette falls to the floor.

"Can I help you?" I say. The words are better than saying nothing.

"Yes, Mr Holleran. I have a case for you. I want you to discover who murdered me."

ABOUT THE AUTHOR

DAVID GREEN grew up reading sci-fi, fantasy and horror. Now, he writes it.

Spending his youth in Manchester, UK, David now lives in Galway, Ireland. New to publishing, despite harbouring ambitions since he could spell his name, David's first work appeared in 2020 and has featured in many Black Hare Press anthologies, with his many more Nick Holleran adventures planned.

Bibliography

Ancients Black Hare Press, 2020

Banned Black Hare Press, 2020

Dead Man Walking: A Nick Holleran Book, Black Hare Press, 2020

Lockdown Horror #2 Black Hare Press, 2020

Lockdown Paranormal Romance #1 Black Hare Press, 2020

Passenger 13 Black Hare Press, 2020

Quietus 13 Black Hare Press, 2020

Reign Black Hare Press, 2021

School's In Black Hare Press, 2020

Wetware Black Hare Press, 2020

Zero Hour 2113 Black Hare Press, 2021

Connect

Website: davidgreenwritercom.wordpress.com/

Amazon: amazon.com/author/davidgreenirl

Twitter: @davidgreenwrite

Facebook: @davidgreenwriter

DAVID GREEN

ABOUT THE PUBLISHER

BLACK HARE PRESS is a small, independent publisher based in Melbourne, Australia.

Founded in 2018, our aim has always been to champion emerging authors from all around the globe and offer opportunities for them to participate in speculative fiction and horror short story anthologies.

Connect

Website: *www.blackharepress.com*

Twitter: *@BlackHarePress*

Printed in Poland
by Amazon Fulfillment
Poland Sp. z o.o., Wrocław

63707983R00054